D0535841

Hello, Sparty!

Aimee Aryal

Illustrated by Julie Reynolds
Michigan State University Class of 2004

www.mascotbooks.com

It was a beautiful fall day at
Michigan State University.

Sparty was on his way to
Spartan Stadium to watch
a football game.

Sparty walked in front of
Beaumont Tower.

A professor passing by said,
"Hello, Sparty!"

Sparty passed by the Main Library.

Some students outside waved,
"Hello, Sparty!"

Sparty walked through the
Beal Botanical Gardens.

A couple sitting on a bench
said, "Hello, Sparty!"

Sparty walked over to
the Breslin Center.

He ran into the basketball coach there.
The coach yelled, "See you
next basketball season, Sparty!"

It was almost time for the football game.
As Sparty walked to the stadium, he
passed by some alumni.

The alumni remembered Sparty from their
days at Michigan State.
They said, "Hello, again, Sparty!"

Finally, Sparty arrived at
Spartan Stadium.

As he ran onto the football field,
the crowd cheered, "Let's go, State!"

Sparty watched the game from
the sidelines and cheered for the team.

The Spartans scored six points!
The quarterback shouted,
"Touchdown, Sparty!"

At halftime, the Spartan Marching Band performed on the field.

Sparty and the crowd chanted
"Go Green, Go White!"

The Michigan State Spartans
won the football game!

Sparty gave the coach a high-five.
The coach said, "Great game, Sparty!"

After the football game,
Sparty was tired. It had been a long day
at Michigan State University.

He walked home and climbed into bed.

Goodnight, Sparty!

For Anna and Maya,
and all of Sparty's little fans. ~ AA

To all of the MSU students who have portrayed Sparty
over the years and to the Schweitzer, Reynolds, and Courter families;
especially my Goddaughter Audrey. ~ JR

For information please contact Mascot Books,
P.O. Box 220157, Chantilly, VA 20153-0157.

MICHIGAN STATE, MICHIGAN STATE UNIVERSITY, MICHIGAN STATE SPARTANS,
the SPARTY Mascot, the Block S design, the CONTEMPORARY SPARTAN HELMET design,
BEAUMONT TOWER, the SPARTAN STATUE, SPARTANS, GO GREEN-GO WHITE and STATE
are Trademarks of Michigan State University. and are used under license.

ISBN: 1-932888-01-2

Printed in the United States.

www.mascotbooks.com

Title List

Team	Book Title	Author	Team	Book Title	Author
Baseball			**Pro**		
			Football		
Boston Red Sox	Hello, Wally!	Jerry Remy	Carolina Panthers	Let's Go, Panthers!	Aimee Aryal
Boston Red Sox	Wally And His Journey	Jerry Remy	Dallas Cowboys	How 'Bout Them Cowboys!	Aimee Aryal
	Through Red Sox Nation!		Green Bay Packers	Go, Packres, Go!	Aimee Aryal
New York Yankees	Let's Go, Yankees!	Yogi Berra	Kansas City Chiefs	Let's Go, Chiefs!	Aimee Aryal
New York Mets	Hello, Mr. Met!	Rusty Staub	Minnesota Vikings	Let's Go, Vikings!	Aimee Aryal
St. Louis Cardinals	Hello, Fredbird!	Ozzie Smith	New York Giants	Let's Go, Giants!	Aimee Aryal
Philadelphia Phillies	Hello, Phillie Phanatic!	Aimee Aryal	New England Patriots	Let's Go, Patriots!	Aimee Aryal
Chicago Cubs	Let's Go, Cubs!	Aimee Aryal	Seattle Seahawks	Let's Go, Seahawks!	Aimee Aryal
Chicago White Sox	Let's Go, White Sox!	Aimee Aryal	Washington Redskins	Hail To The Redskins!	Aimee Aryal
Cleveland Indians	Hello, Slider!	Bob Feller			
			Coloring Book		
			Dallas Cowboys	How 'Bout Them Cowboys!	Aimee Aryal
College					
Alabama	Hello, Big Al!	Aimee Aryal	Michigan State	Hello, Sparty!	Aimee Aryal
Alabama	Roll Tide!	Ken Stabler	Minnesota	Hello, Goldy!	Aimee Aryal
Arizona	Hello, Wilbur!	Lute Olsen	Mississippi	Hello, Colonel Rebel!	Aimee Aryal
Arkansas	Hello, Big Red!	Aimee Aryal	Mississippi State	Hello, Bully!	Aimee Aryal
Auburn	Hello, Aubie!	Aimee Aryal	Missouri	Hello, Truman!	Todd Donoho
Auburn	War Eagle!	Pat Dye	Nebraska	Hello, Herbie Husker!	Aimee Aryal
Boston College	Hello, Baldwin!	Aimee Aryal	North Carolina	Hello, Rameses!	Aimee Aryal
Brigham Young	Hello, Cosmo!	LaVell Edwards	North Carolina St.	Hello, Mr. Wuf!	Aimee Aryal
Clemson	Hello, Tiger!	Aimee Aryal	Notre Dame	Let's Go, Irish!	Aimee Aryal
Colorado	Hello, Ralphie!	Aimee Aryal	Ohio State	Hello, Brutus!	Aimee Aryal
Connecticut	Hello, Jonathan!	Aimee Aryal	Oklahoma	Let's Go, Sooners!	Aimee Aryal
Duke	Hello, Blue Devil!	Aimee Aryal	Oklahoma State	Hello, Pistol Pete!	Aimee Aryal
Florida	Hello, Albert!	Aimee Aryal	Penn State	Hello, Nittany Lion!	Aimee Aryal
Florida State	Let's Go, 'Noles!	Aimee Aryal	Penn State	We Are Penn State!	Joe Paterno
Georgia	Hello, Hairy Dawg!	Aimee Aryal	Purdue	Hello, Purdue Pete!	Aimee Aryal
Georgia	How 'Bout Them Dawgs!	Vince Dooley	Rutgers	Hello, Scarlet Knight!	Aimee Aryal
Georgia Tech	Hello, Buzz!	Aimee Aryal	South Carolina	Hello, Cocky!	Aimee Aryal
Illinois	Let's Go, Illini!	Aimee Aryal	So. California	Hello, Tommy Trojan!	Aimee Aryal
Indiana	Let's Go, Hoosiers!	Aimee Aryal	Syracuse	Hello, Otto!	Aimee Aryal
Iowa	Hello, Herky!	Aimee Aryal	Tennessee	Hello, Smokey!	Aimee Aryal
Iowa State	Hello, Cy!	Amy DeLashmutt	Texas	Hello, Hook 'Em!	Aimee Aryal
James Madison	Hello, Duke Dog!	Aimee Aryal	Texas A & M	Howdy, Reveille!	Aimee Aryal
Kansas	Hello, Big Jay!	Aimee Aryal	UCLA	Hello, Joe Bruin!	Aimee Aryal
Kansas State	Hello, Willie!	Dan Walter	Virginia	Hello, CavMan!	Aimee Aryal
Kentucky	Hello, Wildcat!	Aimee Aryal	Virginia Tech	Hello, Hokie Bird!	Aimee Aryal
Louisiana State	Hello, Mike!	Aimee Aryal	Virginia Tech	Yea, It's Hokie Game Day!	Frank Beamer
Maryland	Hello, Testudo!	Aimee Aryal	Wake Forest	Hello, Demon Deacon!	Aimee Aryal
Michigan	Let's Go, Blue!	Aimee Aryal	West Virginia	Hello, Mountaineer!	Aimee Aryal
			Wisconsin	Hello, Bucky!	Aimee Aryal

NBA

Dallas Mavericks	Let's Go, Mavs!	Mark Cuban

Kentucky Derby

Kentucky Derby	White Diamond Runs For The Roses	Aimee Aryal

More great titles coming soon!

info@mascotbooks.com